For Uma, my little penguin

ATHENEUM BOOKS FOR YOUNG READERS
An imprint of Simon & Schuster Children's Publishing Division
1230 Avenue of the Americas, New York, New York 10020
ATHENEUM BOOKS FOR YOUNG READERS is a registered trademark
of Simon & Schuster, Inc.
Atheneum logo is a trademark of Simon & Schuster, Inc.
For information about special discounts for bulk purchases, please
contact Simon & Schuster Special Sales at 1-866-506-1949 or
business@simonandschuster.com.
The Simon & Schuster Speakers Bureau can bring authors to your
live event. For more information or to book an event, contact the
Simon & Schuster Speakers Bureau at 1-866-248-3049 or visit
our website at www.simonspeakers.com.
Design by Ann Bobco
The text for this book is set in Times New Roman MT Std.

The illustrations for this book are rendered in watercolor and pencil.
Manufactured in China
0214 SCP
First Edition
10 9 8 7 6 5 4 3 2 1
Library of Congress Cataloging-in-Publication Data
Judge, Lita.
Flight school / by Lita Judge. — 1st. ed.
p.   cm.
Summary: Little Penguin, who has the "soul of an eagle," enrolls in
flight school.
ISBN 978-1-4424-8177-0 (hardcover)
ISBN 978-1-4424-8178-7 (eBook)
[1. Penguins—Fiction. 2. Flight—Fiction.] I. Title.
PZ7.J894Fl 2014
[E]—dc23   2012046161

FLIGHT SCHOOL

by LITA JUDGE

A
atheneum
Atheneum Books for Young Readers   New York - London - Toronto - Sydney - New Delhi

"I was hatched to fly," said Penguin.
"When do classes start?"

"But you, dear, are a penguin," Teacher replied.

"Undeniable," said Penguin, "but I have the soul of an eagle."

Teacher and Flamingo weren't so sure, but they let Penguin stay.

"Like this . . .
flip, flap, flap.
And
up, up, up!"

Flight practice started
immediately.

Penguin and the other birdies practiced for weeks.

At last all the birdies were cleared for their first flight. One by one they took to the wind.

And then it was Penguin's turn.

"I'm sorry, birdie," said Teacher. "Penguins just aren't built to fly."

How can this be true? thought Penguin.
In my heart I live on the wind.

But as he watched his classmates fly high above,
he knew it was time to go home.

Penguin was too brokenhearted to even wave good-bye. His teachers didn't know what to do.

FLIGHT SCHOOL
WE TEACH
BIRDS TO FLY

Then Flamingo had an idea.

"Wait!"

"Let's try again."

Flip, flap.

Flip, flap, flap . . .

And up, up, up!

Suddenly Penguin was soaring
above the sea and the clouds.

Penguin was right. He *did* have the soul of an eagle.

He'd just needed a little help with
the technical parts.

But however he felt inside,

he still had the body

of a little,

round . . .

penguin.

But Penguin didn't care.
He had soared on the wind,
just as he had done in
his dreams.

He left flight school a happy little penguin.

It wasn't long before he came back.

"My friend Ostrich
has the soul of a swallow."

Eeep!